Changes

Way Beyond the Sky, Where Dragons Rule, Volume 6

Jeri Andrew

Published by Jeri Andrew, 2023.

CHANGES

First edition. November 8, 2023.

ISBN: 979-8223446125

Written by Jeri Andrew.

Table of Contents

To Drew, there would be no series without you!

in loving memory of Jenni Devlin, taken far too young through the carelessness of others. Gone but not forgotten, always in our hearts...

Chapter 1

AlaHanDrea had a sudden feeling of dread wash over her .. something was wrong... Something was bad wrong.

"Chief, please, you will have to excuse me, something's wrong back home and I need to get there as fast as I can....

I Will be back soon, I promise you that!" She vanished before the chief could respond...

AlaHanDrea had her shields up when she arrived, unsure of what she was going to find, but positive that something was really wrong!

Torches were lit, the ground fire was blazing, as drummers sat around it, mindlessly pounding a steady beat, while musicians added their melodies to the mix.

A party was in full swing, but everyone seemed kind of dazed.

AlaHanDrea spotted a cocoon attached to a tree, then spotted another one... And another...

She ripped the first one open...

"Mitchin! What are YOU doing in a cocoon? Mitchin!" She yelled, shaking him by his shoulders....

"AlaHanDrea! Oh, Thank GOD you are here! We have to help them! It's the Bonner sisters! The are pure evil! I've never experienced an evil like those 4 girls!" Mitchin explained.

"Who are they, Mitchin?"

"They came in with the last refugees. They approached camp playing flutes... The next thing I knew, I was spun up in a cocoon!"

"Jax!" AlaHanDrea yelled, summoning Mr Jax, as she tore open the rest of the cocoons, finding George, Isabel, Braynar, Keithen, Brian, Paulio, Franklon and a couple of other members of the royal guard..

"Mr. Jax.... Please tell me why you transported the Bonner sisters to Taurus 9?"

"I'm not sure what you're talking about."

"Never mind, I already have my answer, you're under their spell! I can smell it on you!" AlaHanDrea told him.

"Spell? Me?" Jax was confused as to what she meant, believing himself to be immune to spells.

"Yes, you! You're under a spell! The Bonner sisters are pure evil, whatever that is."

Jax looked confused, "AlaHanDrea, you don't know what evil is."

"Looks that way, Captain Obvious." The young queen's sarcasm was more than obvious.

"Mitchin, I think this is your department," Jax said, passing the buck.

"Evil, well, it's profoundly immoral and wicked, especially when regarded as a supernatural force... it's an opposition to God as well as something unsuitable or inferior. There are 3 types of evil, Moral evil, natural evil and metaphysical evil.

Basically, evil is a term used to describe something that brings about harmful, painful and unpleasant effects. Moral evil, is evil human beings volitionally and intentionally originate, and it's examples are their cruel, vicious, and unjust thoughts and actions, such as murder.

Natural evil is evil which occurs independently of human thoughts and actions, but which still causes pain and suffering and it refers to quakes volcanos, storms, droughts, diseases, etc...

Metaphysical evil, referrals to spiritual evil.

All things opposing God and Creation are evil," Mitchum explained.

"Who is the God of Evil?"

"There is no God of Evil, there is only one God and he is the opposite of evil. There is, however, the Prince of darkness, a fallen Angel by the name of Lucifer, now, he is pure evil!"

"He is? Well, I guess I'd better break our date then, thanks for the heads up!" She teased.

"Ha Ha, Very funny AlaHanDrea." Jax told her.

"So, what about sex parties, are sex parties evil? Ya know, like the one starting to go on all around us right now?" She asked.

"Huh? What?" Mitchin asked, then looked all around.

"I don't see anyone under aged and everyone seems to be willing participants, I see nothing evil here, but, can we visit later? Things are just starting to get good!" Mitchin asked her....

"Ya, I don't know about y'all, but it's party time!" Jax said, as he went to find him a spot to be....

AlaHanDrea just shook her head and vanished. She had work to do and it was obvious she wasn't getting anywhere by staying where she was!

"Danalli, are you home, baby?" AlaHanDrea hollered out as she entered his lair.

"Ya, I'm over here, watching some movies from the human sectors. Come over and snuggled with me," he said, then put some chocolate candies in his mouth.

"Are you feeling alright, baby?" She asked.

"Ya, I'm feeling pretty good. Healix showed me inside of the eggs! One looks to be humanoid... The other two are dragons, for sure. The girl is a dragon," he said with pride.

She went over and laid down with him for a minute after all.

"This feels really good, sweetheart," she admitted.

"So, tell me about the islands..." Danalli asked.

"Well, the monsters name is Millie, she's some kind of a water dragon. I showed her how to shift and introduced her to the natives in people form, then told them who she really was. But then, I had to leave, because I sensed trouble back here."

"Ya, me too, that's why I'm hold up here in this cave like this."

"Wise decision, sweetheart. Gotta keep the babies safe. Wanna make some more? She asked with a naughty grin....

Danalli leaned up, gazed deeply in her eyes, kissing her with love and passion.... Then stopped.

"I can't believe I'm saying this, but, not tonight, baby. I mean, I love you with my whole heart... I honestly do.... And I love sex! Especially with you... But I need to get these three hatched first, before we go making any more..."

"Ya, I guess you're right about that! Kinda sux that sex makes babies and can't be turned off until you're ready for babies..."

"Ya, but that would mean interfering with the natural order of things and we just don't do that." Danalli told her.

"I suppose your right, baby. Listen, as great as this feels, I've gotta go see to these Bonner sisters... They had your whole family cocooned! Time to go kick some alien butt!

Make them think twice before messing with my dragons again!" She told him.

"Well, go get them, girl! Go teach them some manners like only you can do! I have total faith in you!"

"Thank you, baby. Well, stay in here and stay safe. If these bitches find out you're my love and are carrying babies, they will use you against me... so, please just stay here.

I'll see if I can send some food back," she told him, then kissed him goodbye and left to go find those girls...

"Hello Merrill," AlaHanDrea said as she entered Merrill's work shop.

"AlaHanDrea! I didn't see you come in, come on in, have a seat... can I get you something to drink?" the suspicious wizard asked his unexpected visitor.

"Merrill, we have some interesting refugees on the planet. Because of them, Mitchin was explaining evil to me, and I'm still confused."

"Confused in what way?" He asked.

"Are you considered evil?"

"Well, now, that's not a simple subject. I don't consider myself to be evil, but most folks consider those I work and play with to be evil. The ones I follow are considered to be evil."

"But, you helped save and restore me..."

"Being on the dark side, doesn't mean I'm incapable of doing good things. Just like being on the light side doesn't mean someone is incapable of doing bad things."

"Oh. Well, do you know the Bonner sisters?"

"Ya, we've met. I dabble in darkness, those girls are straight up pure evil! Incapable of doing good things. I don't much care for them. They didn't seem to be very fond of me, either," Merrill explained.

"What needs to be done about them?"

"I'm not sure I know what you mean."

"Merrill, I like to think of you and I as having a special bond... more than just friends... after all, you helped give me life again," she told the old wizard...

"Well, thank you sweetheart. I appreciate that..." he told her.

"Thanks, uh.... you keep looking at my breasts...."

"Oh, sorry... ya, I'm a dirty old man...."

"Really? I prefer to think of you more as a sexy senior citizen..." she teased.

"Oh, hey, I kinda like that!" Merrill replied with a grin.

"You're still looking at my breasts..."

"Well, they are quite nice, AlaHanDrea. Anyway, I'm just an only ol perv, what do you expect?"

She opened her top, "you can see them better now, go ahead, take a good look! I'm putting them away now, think we can get your mind on something besides my breasts?"

"Well, o.k, if you insist, but they are really nice!"

She walked over to him and put his face between them for a moment, then stepped back, "how about now? Can we talk about the girls now?"

"Sure. That was very nice, thank you! O.k. The Bonner Sisters.... What do you want done with them?" He asked.

"I'm not really sure yet. I know that I do not want you on their side... I want you loyal to me... completely and totally loyal to me!"

"I see."

"Merrill, I'm probably the most powerful creature you will ever meet.... Why wouldn't you be and remain completely loyal to me? The Bonner sisters derive their power from Lucifer. I derive power from no one, I am power!"

"You make some very good points."

"I won't tolerate betrayal, Merrill...."

She walked over to him, stared him in the eyes, then kissed him the way a woman kisses a man she wants to melt in passions heat.... He was stunned.... So, she kissed him again, this time, placing his hand on her breast.

45 minutes later.... "I'm going for a quick swim, care to join me?"

"Right behind you, sweetheart!"

She splashed him playfully as he got in the natural pool.....

They played in the water splashing around, having a pretty good time.

"Wow, I didn't know I still had it in me...." He admitted to her. "2 times And once in the water, no less! I'm impressed with myself! You bring out the best in me."

"Oh ya? Well, your turn, kiss me! " she instructed... then hopped up out of the pool. He followed her out of of the water, slipping a robe on.

"You are stunningly beautiful, AlaHanDrea! Amazingly so. I never dreamed I could have you! Is this a one time thing, or...." He asked, then kissed her.

"I'm not into one on one relationships, Merrill. But, I do expect you to be mine. You can have sex with whoever you want, but when it comes right down to it, I want you to be mine, all mine. 100%. Betray me and you will beg for death!

I want you to be MY wizard! As long as you are MY wizard and are loyal to me, you can have sex with me from time to time. "

So, we're having an affair? Hmmm, I like that! I like that a lot! You got yourself a deal, baby cakes! I will follow you anywhere!"

"One revision.... You can have sex with anyone you want, except, the Bonner sisters... or, anyone like them or associated with them in any way."

"Woman, you've got yourself a wizard! One more time to seal the deal?"he asked with a naughty wink...

"Well, of course! Come here, big guy!" She said, as she laid sideways in a hammock....

Chapter 2

"Hello, we, are looking for Queen AlaHanDrea. Are you her?" Mellie Mae asked.

""Hello, Mellie Mae. Yes, I'm her. what do you want?"

"Wow, you already know our names...

I'm afraid we've gotten off on the wrong foot. We'd like to apologize.

We never meant to get on your wrong side.

Quite the opposite.

We want more than anything to become friends with you!"

"Oh, really?"

"Yes, really."

"You sure have a funny way of showing it," the teen queen said, with sarcasm in her voice.

"Look, the last thing we want, is to be enemies with you. Please, tell us how we can fix this?" Amelia asked.

"This is My Planet!

I'm head bitch, no one is above me!

These are MY dragons!

My Bears!

My Creatures!

Stay here, and y'all are my 4 evil bitches!" AlaHanDrea said with a smirk on her face. "

"George and Isabel rule the planet... I rule George, Isabel, and everyone on it."

"So we've heard. Would you not love to have 4 friends as powerful as you?" Emilie asked.

"You're kidding, right? What makes you think your even half as powerful as me?"

"Kinda full of yourself, aren't you?" Amelia asked her.

"A creature has not been born that has more power than me!" AlaHanDrea had 3 of them cocooned before they could say don't.

"Well, Amelia, what say you now?" The teen queen asked her.

Amalia got a strange look on her face...

"What's the matter Amelia, magic on the blitz?

Your magic has no power over me, girl.

You, have no power over me!

HE, has no power over me!

You see, I worship the creator. Why would I want to follow number 2 when number one is better?"

I don't do second place..."

"O.k., Queen AlaHanDrea, you've had your fun, let my sister's go."

"Even together, your magic has no effect on me. Get used to it."

"O.K, fine, now do you see why we want to be your friends? Who in their right mind would want to be your enemy?"

"Psychology doesn't work on me either."

"Well, what does work on you, girl?" Amelia teased...

"Honesty. Absolute honesty, since, I already know the truth, anyway."

"There, your sisters are free. Go ahead, give it your best shot..."

"Girls, stop. Just stop. It's having no effect on her at all. Just stop. So, AlaHanDrea, friends or foe?" Emilie asked her.

"How would I know. I don't know you well enough to answer that question."

"Well, would you like to get know us better?"

"What I would like, is for you to keep your paws off of MY Creatures! Go Jack with the humans.... No one cares and from what I hear, they just love evil ..."

"You don't care if we mess with the humans?"

"Well, I mean, don't go crazy or anything, but ya, go live in the human sectors, just stay the hell off my Islands.

You know what? The southern hemisphere of this planet would be a great place for you ladies to get settled down.

It's much too far away for the northern hemisphere to interact with. I know no one from down under ... why don't you go down there and rule the roost, bowing only to me and no other?

Of course, showing George and Isabel the respect world leaders deserve, but bowing only to me... Loyal only to me?"

"You want we should worship you?" Mellie Mae asked.

"That's not what I said, tho, I suspect I'm every bit as powerful as your dark Prince, if not even more so...."

"Yes, but can you make others more powerful?" Amelia asked.

"Well, of course I can allow access to some of my power...."

Everyone was startled by a sudden clap of thunder.

AlaHanDrea got very excited and hurried over to her favorite hill, while her guest headed for cover...

AlaHanDrea didn't have long to wait for the storm to reach close enough to be summoned.

The sisters watched in amazement as the teen queen called the electricity from the storm... Absorbing lightening bolt after lightening bolt...

She stood on the hill, arms stretched towards the heavens, singing to call the storm, which obeyed without hesitation ...

The sisters watched her whole body light up as the lightening entered her...

Once AlaHanDrea had her fill, she gently blew air at the storm and sent it on its way.

When she returned to the girls, they were on their knees, bowed down in worship mode.

"Rise," AlaHanDrea told them.

"Please forgive us, we didn't know. We had no idea! We've never encountered a creature such as you before!" Mellie Mae told her.

Emilie spoke up, " You see, we can't approach the prince of darkness like we can approach you! We can just walk right up to you, like a regular person.

But not so with God or with The Prince..."

"Because I am in the flesh..."

"Oh, well, right," Amelia said ...

"So, tell me, friends, what made you go to the dark side?" AlaHanDrea asked them.

"Persecution. We are shifters, dragons... We needed the power in order to survive. With God, you have to use what you're born with,"

Emilie explained.

"Makes sense to me. He will forgive you, ya know. He still loves you. He would actually celebrate if you were to return to Him. You see, you were born His.

You weren't supposed to have to choose, you were already His. You just don't know how to access His power... and... your prince of darkness is a liar that feeds on your fear.

I'd never make you choose between me or God. To choose me is to also choose God.

How can you possibly love me and not also Love He who Creates all?"

"I can already tell that life on this planet is going to be so different!" Amelia said.

"Now, don't go thinking your Prince of darkness is going to just give you up without a fight..." AlaHanDrea warned them.

She cocooned Mellie Mae. " Don't be afraid, this isn't going to hurt you a bit. I'm just showing you something, a little sampling. It's going to be just a few minutes so while we're waiting why don't you demonstrate some of the things that you can do with your powers, like this flute music of yours... come on, let me hear it," she instructed.

The sisters played their best, it had no effect on AlaHanDrea, whatsoever.

"Pretty music." AlaHanDrea had some flutes appear, floating in the air, playing themselves. The sisters were in a trance in moments. She snapped Amelia out of it and plugged her ears so she could observe.

Amelia was in Awe!

She stopped the music and brought the other girls out of their trance.

AlaHanDrea had the girls explode some boulders, she put them back together again.

Then, the teen queen blew colder than cold ice flames, followed by fireballs she threw from her hands.

Then, AlaHanDrea shrank herself very tiny, then back, then shifted to appear as a dragon, then back again.

The girls applauded her!

They showed her some of the skill seeing through crystal balls ... AlaHanDrea Made a viewing screen appear and played their thoughts and memories up on the screen!

"And your power is natural. It's just yours. Not borrowed with a price tag... You were born this way... I'm in awe of you!

You're right, tho, AlaHanDrea, the prince isn't just going to sit still while we shift to the other side... Emily said. "The shadow people will be coming for us..."

"You mean those guys over there in that cage?" AlaHanDrea pointed over to a clear sided box full of shadows, growling, snarling and trying desperately to get free.

"How'd you do that?" Amelia asked.

"It's not hard. Darkness has no power over the light. Want to see something really cool that will make the shadows really go nuts?" She asked.

"Sure!" They said in Unison.

"Sarafina! Oh, Sarafina, may I please see you for a moment?"

Bright lights and ground fog startled the girls! They hid their faces from the light at first, then slowly opened them to see a real angel standing in their midst.

"Thank you for coming Sarafina. I believe you already know these girls...."

"Yes, I do. How are you ladies?" The beautiful angel asked them.

"Wow! Oh wow! You are like, a real Angel from Heaven!?! Oh wow!" Amelia said.

"Yes, I am."

The shadows locked in the transparent box we're going nuts in the presence of an angel...

"Well, what do we have here?" Sarafina asked, as she casually strolled towards the cage.

She held up her hands and vanquished every last one of the trapped shadow people....

"Is that what you called me here for, sweetie?" Sarafina asked AlaHanDrea.

"Yes, and thank you very much. I love you, Sarafina."

"I love you, too, AlaHanDrea. Call me if you need me!" She said, then vanished.

"From the bottom of our hearts, we apologize to you! We were so wrong about you! We were so wrong!" Amy cried.

"You didn't know. Well, I think it's time to release Mellie Mae... Are you ready to see your new improved sister, girls?"

AlaHanDrea asked them.

Without waiting for an answer, AlaHanDrea flipped her hand in the direction of the cocoon, causing it to slowly rip open.

Mellie Mae stepped out, shook herself off, then said, "wow! I feel great!"

Her sisters were absolutely flabbergasted! She no longer had any body fat! Gone was about 70 unneeded pounds of excess fat ..

Her skin glowed, her hair was fuller, longer, richer in color, wavy with curles on the bottom.... Her eyes were brighter, breasts were perky, as well as larger... Her cheeks were rosey and she had small wings like AlaHanDrea's....

But, most of all, her magic was much stronger! And she could feel it...

AlaHanDrea made a full length mirror appear so she could check herself out.

"Wow! Is that Me?"

"Ya, that's really you!"

She fell down in front of AlaHanDrea and kissed the tops of her feet, with tears of joy running down her cheeks.

"Anything you want from me, anything at all, I am your loyal servant! My Queen, oh, my precious queen!" Mellie Mae cried....

AlaHanDrea helped her up on her feet, helped to wipe her tears away and said, "does your dark Prince do anything like this for you?"

She had won their hearts and knew it.

"Ya know girls, I'm not perfect. None of us are. But I do try my best. That's all I ask of you girls, that you always just try your best! But, it starts with rebuking Lucifer and all that he stands for. Can you do that?

Now, what was your purpose in cocooning the other dragons? What was that trance all about? What were trying to accomplish, that I interrupted?"

"We were just having some fun. We put the royals away, ya know... like putting the police away..

We didn't hurt them any. And all our music did was to put them in a dreamy, feel good place....

We were just trying to have a little fun! We weren't trying to hurt anybody, honest!"

"From this day forward, you leave my dragons and my creatures alone! You leave my humans alone!

Chapter 3

Music was one of AlaHanDrea's favorite parts of life on Taurus 9. The evening fires were such an awesome way to close a day...

The teen queen was relaxing in a big double hammock, enjoying the evening breeze with music floating effortlessly through the air, as if sent to her as a gift ....

"Pssst, over here, it's me, can I come over to see you, please?" She recognized the male voice....

"Yes, Merrill, it's so good to see you, what a pleasant surprise!"

"You look so comfortable, I almost hate to disturb you. Are you sure no one will see us?" Merrill asked

"Why, are you ashamed to be seen with me?" She asked, teasingly.

"Well, of course not! It's just that affairs are usually kept quiet," he explained, blushing deep red.

The teen queen smiled and said, "I put a cloaking spell over us. No one can see us." She sat up, looking deeply into his eyes.

Merrill smiled and said, "I haven't been able to get you out of my mind. I'm even dreaming about you...

About being with you... About how you feel...

And I had to come see you again.

I just had to," he admitted.

She put her hands on his face and kissed him so sweetly, she took his breath away. He put his arms around her and kissed her with unbridled passion.

She loved the power she had over males...

As hard as Merrill tried to fight it, he fell deeply in love with AlaHanDrea. He tried telling himself not to... But he fell and he fell hard ..

"Girl, what do you want with an old man like me, when you've got every young, built, handsome male in the land chasing after you?" He asked, as they laid breathless in the hammock.

"They aren't you." She told him.

"But, you and I can't be, not like what you need, like you deserve.
I'm human.

I may be a wizard, but I'm still human.

I grow older with every passing day.

You age so slowly, it's as if time stands still for you."

"Exactly. And you are an awesome creature, for a human..." She teased. "Why shouldn't I be able to enjoy you while you're here?
Maybe I will forbid you to die!"

"You can do that?"

"Sure I can. I don't want those that I love to die. I won't let them!"

"Oh sweetie, wow, you really are a powerful creature. But, what happens when they are supposed to be dead, but still live?"

"Then they live on!"

"No, I mean, do they continue to age?" He asked, with a touch of fear in his voice.

"I dunno, you tell me."

"AlaHanDrea, there are some things you shouldn't interfere with, I think that natural death is probably on the top of that list."

"Tell me that when your time comes and you're not ready for it to.
You were ready, you were really ready, sure you'd lived all that you could... before...

before you worked with a watcher, side by side to save my life...

Before you became friends with dragons and began to hang out with shape shifting creatures... before you had sex with me...

are you still ready to die, old man?

Or do you want more?"

"Of course I want more."

"That's good, because I already gave you more."

"What do you mean, you already gave me more?"

"Merrill, the first time we did it, you tried to pass. I stopped you. You are on your extra time now. Right now. This minute, you are undead.

I got to regenerate, but I know first hand that dead kinda sux.

I don't know how to make you regenerate, like you did for me, but I returned the favor and made you not be dead."

"I'm dead?"

"No, are you not listening? You were dead, I made you not dead."

"I died."

"Yes, you did."

"I had sex with you, and I died."

"Well, not the first time we did it, but, I guess you were a bit old for 3 times in a row. But that's o.k, I didn't let you die!

See?

Now we're even!

Well, as close as we can get to being even.

I can't exactly grow you a new body."

"Please don't take this wrong, but I think I'm going to need to take some time to think."

"Oh, I'm sure. Take all of the time you need to take, I'm sure it comes as a great shock.

Don't you remember Me blowing air into your body?"

"Yes, actually, I do remember that!

That's when I died?"

"No, that's when you came back to life."

"Wow, I was just gone and never even knew it happened!"

"Oh no, you knew it. You looked me right in the eye and told me that you weren't ready, apologized, then died. So, I fixed it for you! And you're still here!"

"Oh my!

I remember that now!

I did die!

And it hurt!"

"This is your new life! Your second life!

For as long as I live, you live also...

You and I share a special bond now!

Go!

Live!

Come back to me when things feel right again. But for now, go enjoy being alive again!

Do something good with this second life!

Have some fun!

Explore!

Just please, keep in touch!

By the way, how many years have you lived so far?" she asked, almost afraid to hear the answer.

Merrill smiled and said, "I'm a spry young man of nearly300.

Human wizards do live much longer than typical humans, much longer, but still, not as long as dragons, or those who can regenerate."

"So, that's why you thought you were ready to die, you already lived nearly three centuries... well, please keep in touch... let me know how the whole undead thing works out for you! And remember, do no harm, or, I may have to take it back..."

Merrill vanished before her last words were spoken.

"AlaHanDrea! Are you around?" Isabel called out.

AlaHanDrea could hear Isabel calling from under the water of the pool.

She swam up to the surface to see what was going on.

"Oh, here you are! I'll get you a robe..." Isabel told her.

"Thanks Izzy, wow, I needed that swim."

"Is everything o.k? Isabel asked.

"Ya, it's supposed to be a secret, but I'm having an affair with the wizard and..."

"Wait, what? O.k, please continue... "

"Well, the first time we did it, he died. Only I didn't want him to die and he didn't want to die, so, I made him not be dead."

"You can do that?"

"Ya, apparently I can. So, I finally told him today, since, he didn't seem to remember. He took off to go think about things and all.... Anyway, this is the first time I've done anything like this.

It would be a very bad thing for word to get out that I can do this, so, you may want to keep this to yourself.

Anyway, I don't know exactly what kind of effect this is going to have on him.

We need to keep an eye on him... so, I'm putting a spy eye on him so we can monitor his actions. I just thought someone else besides me should know this..."

"Thanks for telling me. uh, the reason I stopped by, is because the Bonner sisters are a bit of a handful! So, you made us Immune to their magic?"

"Yes, I did do that."

"Great! But, I take it, you only made the royal circle immune?"

"Yes."

"Well, thanks for that! Those girls sure do love to party! Can you restrict their magic?"

"I dunno, I can try."

"Would you, please? The mines are being neglected."

"Oh! O.k. I'll see what I can do. We can't have the mines not producing. Every bit of balance comes from those mines producing! The gem trade with the humans is what maintains the balance!

I can see why it's stressful for everyone to be partying all the time.... I'll have a chat with the girls!" The young queen replied.

"By the way, great job with Mellie Mae!" Isabell commented.

"Thanks! She's much healthier now!" AlaHanDrea was feeling proud of herself for the changes made in the young woman.

"She's actually the first overweight Dragon I've ever seen!" Isabel admitted.

"Ya know, maybe it would be a good idea for the girls to spend some time in Dragon state. I think they spent way too much time as humans!" AlaHanDrea suggested.

"Good point. Yeah, some Dragon time would be good for them, can you make it happen please?" Isabel agreed.

"Sure!

Bonner sisters!" AlaHanDrea summoned them.

"Yes, AlaHanDrea? You wanted to see us?" Mellie Mae asked when the sisters popped in.

"Yes. Transform please. Shift to Dragon for me right now please." AlaHanDrea ordered.

"Oh, o.k." they all three agreed, shifting right away.

"Okay you're going to stay this way now until I say otherwise. You need some time being your natural selves. Being in Human state may come naturally to you, because you've done it for so much of your lives, but, you are dragons first and foremost and it's about time you live as such. This is not permanent, but I do feel it is necessary and so does Queen Isabel."

"But, but, AlaHanDrea!" the girls protested.

"No buts about it! You girls are a tad bit out of control and you need to get back to your roots... Remember who you really are... find out who you really are.

Living on a planet that forbid you to be who you are was a bad thing for you ... it's not your fault! You didn't make it that way... you did the best you could with what you had to work with... but... things are different here. It is high time you learn who you are, what you are and learn to live as such. And... I can't think of a better gift to give you! Understand that this is a gift of love... Of love for you and of love for your fellow dragons."

"As much as I hate to admit it, She's Right!" Emilia told her sisters.

"Thank you, AlaHanDrea. By the way, you have a very lovely name, but it's also a very long name...." Emilia commented.

"No, not really. You are saying all three of my names all run together as one name!" The young queen explained.

"Really?"

"Yes, my name is Ala Han Drea. Ala and Han are predominately male names, the angels named me. My name means, 'God's special messenger, brave and strong warrior, protector of all!"

"Oh, wow! That's so beautiful! May we call you Alaha?"

Isabel and AlaHanDrea looked at each other, the pain in the eyes was obvious...

"Did we say something wrong?" Amy asked.

"No, no, I had a baby named Alaha, she is no more."

"Oh, we are so sorry! We didn't know!"

"No, it's o.k. it really is o.k. many refer to me as Alaha. Some call me Drea. Others call me baby girl... I answer to it all."

"AlaHanDrea! You home?" Braynar called out.

Braynar, Keithen and Danalli came walking into camp. Danalli's pouch was getting quite large!

"Ah, here you are. AlaHanDrea, Danalli won't tell us who the mother is, can you get it out of him? I mean, it's obvious he has eggs growing...." Keithen asked.

"It's not for me to tell. He's your brother. I suppose if he wants you to know that he and I are about to become parents, then he will tell you that he and I are about to become parents... But until he's ready to tell you that he and I are having babies, 3 babies, 2 boys and a girl, then you'll just have to guess if I'm the mother or not to his and my 3 babies...." She teased.... Danalli walked over to AlaHanDrea so she could kiss his face.

The Stunned silence was almost deafening!

"He's such a beautiful dragon with babies in his pouch," she said, caressing his nose.

Isabel just stood there, smiling...

"You girls sure do look beautiful tonight," Keithen told the Bonner sisters.

They all just blushed.

"Hey, do y'all wanna go for a fly about? Maybe find some supper?" Keithen asked them.

"Oh, we'd love to!"

"Y'all go on ahead, little bro, I'll catch up with y'all later. Why don't you ask Brian and Kenneth to join you!" Braynar said to his little brother. Kind of his way of sending an unspoken message to AlaHanDrea.

"Danalli, dude, we'll bring ya back some food!"

Keithen and the girls took off to go meet up with the other guys and go on the hunt.

"Well, I'm going to go back to my lair and lay down awhile!" Danalli said, obviously drained of energy by growing babies.

"O.k., Danalli, get some rest. I'll see you soon," AlaHanDrea said, then kissed him on his snout.

"I think this is my cue to leave, thanks, AlaHanDrea!

Have a good day now..." Isabel told them as she turned to leave.

"So, you and Danalli are having babies. Are you sure one of those eggs isn't mine?" Braynar asked.

"Positive. But, if you'd like to make an egg with me, I'm not going to object," she said, with a wink. "Ah, cmon, Braynar, what's wrong? You said it yourself, I'm far too young for a committed relationship and anyway, you have sex with who ever, when ever, and I don't say a word! Anyway, Danalli and I have been waiting since we were dead together when I was 6."

He didn't say a word, he just threw her over his shoulder like a sack of potatoes and carried her down to his lair, with her laughing all the way....

Chapter 4

Braynar woke up, just before daylight, feeling kind of queezy. He checked the egg to make sure it was o.k. everything seemed just fine.

He began to question his decision to reproduce. It didn't take him very long to realize that he did it feeling territorial over AlaHanDrea. He hadn't really intended to fertilize an egg... But, he did! It was a spotted egg, too!

Still, he wasn't ready to make it public Information yet. Not even to immediate family...

The expectant father decided to go do a fly about and collect up a pit full of food. He knew he wasn't going to be feeling up to going hunting, as the baby absorbed energy from him.

It was best he got his pit good and full.

What he hadn't planned on, was what happened next!

He smelled them, long before he saw them! So, he landed and shifted. That was something he wouldn't be doing very much of soon... Shifting, that is...

He followed the smell until he came up on a hunting party.

The men reeked of sin!

There was about a dozen or so men in the camp, so, Braynar decided to fake being injured, looking for help.

"Sssshhh, I think I heard something! Pipe down fellas, I think I heard someone calling for help! There it is again!" Jeff hollered out at the group of hunters.

"Sounded like it was coming from over that way a bit, come on!" Craig told the others.

"Whoa! Hi there, big fella, we heard you calling for help, are you hurt?" Craig asked Braynar.

"Uh, ya, I seem to have injured my ankle," Braynar told them.

"My, you sure have a deep voice. Here, we'll help you up. Do you think you can stand?" Brad asked him.

"Not sure. It hurts pretty badly."

"O.k. can I get some help over here?"

"O.k. big fella, the three of us are going to try to help you walk, if we can... "

"Let's put him down over there in the big lounger... So, what are you doing way out here all alone?" Jay asked him.

"Hunting. I was hunting. My uh, pantry was nearly empty."

"I see. You have to be careful dude! A big guy like you is liable to attract dragons, or worse!" Jay told him.

"Ya, You're lucky wild animals didn't find you first. Nice crown, you a prince or something?" Jay asked.

"Ya, or something."

"Oh man. Dude, you really gotta be careful! Kidnappers could find you! Fortune seekers..." Brad told him.

"You mean, like you fellas?" Braynar asked him, then laughed. "No one has to kidnap me to find a fortune. All they have to do is ask politely and I'll show them right where it all is."

"You're kidding, right?" Jay asked.

"I never kid about treasure. It looks to be an abandoned mine." Braynar told them.

"And you're just going to show us where it is?" Steve asked him.

"Why not? It's not like I can retrieve all of the gold and jewels all by myself. Why not you guys, something wrong with y'all? There's enough treasure there for a whole lot more than you fellas!"

"Why would a producing mine be abandoned?"

"Maybe the Dragon died... Or moved... I don't know, but I've been watching the place and there's no sign of activity there for quite some time now... Do ya wanna see it or not?"

"Jeff, you and Steve go with him and check it out. We will be close behind, y'all will travel much faster without all of us tagging along. We won't be far behind..." Dan told the guys.

"It's a bit of a journey, any of you fellas into magic?"

"You're joking, right?"

"Ya, I'm real funny that way! It's actually not that far from here. Want to see what's inside of that mine? Here, look at these. I pulled these out only yesterday," he told them, handing them the pouch.

Their eyes almost bulged out when they saw the size of the gem stones and the quality of the gold!

Braynar pulled out quite a few little pouches and tossed them to the guys.

"Y'all can go ahead and keep those, I have plenty more..."

The guys went nuts over the the treasure inside of those pouches...

"Well, what are we waiting for? Let's go see this mine!" Jay said.

Brad fashioned a wheeled litter to pull Braynar... It was almost like a wheel chair wagon sorta thing... Braynar rather liked the contraption.

6 guys wound up going with him, since he was hard to pull... Braynar was a very large man!

""So, how much stuff you guys have that it'll take so long for the others to catch up with us?" Braynar asked them.

"Several wagons, actually. But, they will be right along, don't you worry. So, have you told anyone else about your find?"

"No, not yet. Ya see, I got jilted by my lover. Really broke my heart. Shattered it man, you know what I mean? Found out she's having kids with my brother..."

"Oh, that's rough, dude. That's really rough..."

"Ya, so I just left...

Made myself a camp, decided to stay alone for a bit.

I was chasing some food...That's when I found the cave.

But, to tell ya the truth, I'm not all that interested in treasure right now..." Braynar explained.

"It's not every day we run across a wounded fella giving away a kings fortune of treasure..."

"I'm sure," Braynar agreed.

"Dude, how much further we gotta go?"

"It's actually right through those vines. I'll go first, if you're scared... It'll be kind of hard tho, with my ankle and all."

"I'm not scared!" Jeff said, as he put his head lamp on and grabbed a spot light.

"I'll be right here when y'all get back," Braynar told them.

"I'll stay right here with the big fella," John said.

"Fine, suit yourself," Jeff told him. They weren't gone very long before they came running out of the cave, full of excitement...

"Dude! I've never seen so much treasure in my whole life! It's unreal!"

Don exclaimed, then took off running to tell the others.

"Big guy, you really don't mind us getting all of this treasure?" Bill asked him.

"Why should I mind? It's not doing me any good! Nothing's doing me any good."

"Well, sorry about your troubles dude, but, thanks! Sure you're not going to change your mind?" Joe asked.

"I'm positive."

"Well, I don't know about you, Frank, but I ain't for waiting around!" Joe said as he took off into the cave.

The others followed him. Braynar used his magic to make a body double and made it look very murdered, then put a cloak over himself to appear invisible and stood back behind a bush.

The others weren't far behind...

"Oh, Man! Check this shit out! The guys went and killed the big dude!

How rude! Dude shows us to the treasure and they killed him dead! Looks like Frank's handiwork," Dan commented.

"They are probably already in the mine grabbing up loot! The tracks say they are, anyway. I'm heading in..." Charlie said to the group.

Charlie wasn't gone more than a minute before the others followed him in.

Once they were all inside and down to the "treasure mine", a barred gate quietly closed, locking them all inside.

They were all so enthralled with the treasure, no one noticed at first.

Charlie asked the group, so, who decided to murder the big dude?"

"What are you talking about? He was alive when we left him!"

"Well, go have a look for yourself, some one butchered him up pretty good!"

"No way!

Hey!

Hey!

What's the frickin deal here!

Dudes!

We're locked in!

It was a trap!

It's a trap!!!" Joe called out.

The men could be heard from outside of the cave.

Braynar was laughing to himself at the stupidity greed causes in humans... Then he heard it... The sound of girls crying!

It was coming from the hunters wagons!

Braynar uncovered the first wagon, only to find it full of female children! Human female children... And babies!

He lifted back the cover off of the second wagon only to find that it, too, was full of female babies and children. He was almost afraid to uncover the third wagon...

Much to his relief, It was filled with young women.

"What are y'all doing in those cages?" Braynar asked them.

"Those men stole us. They burned our villages, killed our men and stole us!"

"Oh boy. AlaHànDrea!!!" Braynar called out.

"Yes, my love?"

The women began crying when they saw magic at work. That kind of magic could only mean one thing, dragons!

"I have a donation for your islands!" Braynar told AlaHanDrea.

"Oh wow! Bray, where'd you get them and why are they caged?"

"I found them this way. But, what do I do with them, I can't eat them. I mean, I could eat them, but I choose not to eat them…"

"You're right, they do belong on the islands, but, the islands aren't ready yet.. I guess we take them home with us."

"With us, what am I going to do with a bunch of little humans? " Braynar asked her.

"What am I gonna do with them? Anyway, they are yours, not mine!"

"How do you figure?"

"You found them, they are yours. Actually, I think you rescued them! I hear voices coming from your favorite treasure trap…"

"Ya, it works every time! Humans and their greed!"

"Have they discovered yet that there is no treasure?"

"Not yet… " he laughed…

"O.k. Well, we are wasting daylight. How do you want to transport them? oh, never mind, I'll do it…" AlaHanDrea said, then used her magic for multiple trips until they were all transported.

"O.k., listen up! Big ones, take care of the little ones! Oh boy…. We need help! Leon!!!" AlaHanDrea called out. "Bjorn!!!"

"Well, what do we have here?" Leon asked.

"Rescued humans. We need help, Leon! Bjorn! Please!?!"

Leon and Bjorn both called for their tribes. They divided the girls up between them, only leaving 3 behind. A baby, a girl who looked around

14 years old and a 22 year old. AlaHanDrea made a place for them to sleep, then took off.

"Hello? Is someone there? C'mon, I can smell someone there..." Keithen called out.

"Well, if you can smell me, then why didn't you know it was me?" AlaHanDrea asked him.

"Well, hello, I didn't hear you come in. You're not wearing any clothes."

"I'm not? Well, shame on me! Should I go, then?"

Keithen shifted, stood there, gazing into her eyes as tho he were trying to decide what to do.

"Really Keithen? A beautiful naked woman comes into your lair and you're not sure what to do with her???"

"I know what I want to do," he commented.

"So, what's stopping you? Do you not want to make a baby with me?"

"AlaHanDrea, I love you very much! But, what about my brothers?"

"And what about your brothers? I don't belong to them! You and I used to be very close... tell me you don't want me and I will go."

"Of course I want you! I want you more than anything else in this world!"

AlaHanDrea walked over and crawled up in his bed. He stood there, looking at her for the longest time, then went over and crawled in next to her...

Daylight came way too soon!

"AlaHanDrea, we made a baby..."

"Well good then, that's what I came for. Now, it's even. None of you has something the other doesn't have."

Chapter 5

When AlaHanDrea returned home, Elfen fairies were hard at work, building rooms for the children, deciding that a ground level hut was probably best for the time, because of the baby.

There was a strange chill in the air, the temperature had dropped more than 30° and was still dropping.

No one knew what to do. They had never felt cold before.

The fairies had experience with weather, or, at least their ancestors did... they already anticipated high water, as well as cold, so, they built the hut round, to withstand winds, put it on low stilts with an outer deck all the way around, with a wood burning stove at it's center.

Since the hut was for humans, there was also a wood burning kitchen stove. Everything was in one room, with pony walls dividing the areas, for ease in watching the baby.

The hut was very toddler friendly, while still being appealing to an adolescent and a young adult.

There were also 4 fireplaces built into the outer wall. They were built perfectly at North, East, South and West.....

Part of the hot spring waterfall was enclosed into the Hut as a wonderful source of heated water. One simply stood under the falls to shower.

When the girls first saw the hut, all of the fireplaces didn't really make much sense, but, with the sudden drop in temperature, they made perfect sense.

Broadcast drones were up like never before, to help with the confusion caused by the weather phenomenons.

Other regions of the planet were suffering heat like never before, while cold was quickly coming down on the other parts of the planet.

Thunder off in the distance was unsettling. An approaching storm that already felt worse than anything Taurus 9 and her inhabitants had ever felt before, was headed there way.

The fairies began working even faster, finally stopping and hollering at everyone to take cover in high ground, then fluttered off to their own villages to hunker down.

AlaHanDrea gathered the girls up and headed for Braynar's mountain top lair.

A sudden urgency to find Danalli came over her.

"Y'all wait right here! Don't leave! You'll be safe here. I have to go find Danalli," She instructed, after lighting the fireplaces and torches.

Before she left, she used her magic to put a table full of food near the fireplace.

Terror gripped the girls when they heard the dragon coming their way!

"Don't be afraid, it's me, Braynar, the big guy that saved you from the bad men.

I'm a dragon.

I won't hurt you.

Dragons are people, too. Don't be afraid.

It's just hard for me to shift to man state, because I'm carrying an egg.

Please, just relax, I'm here to protect you.

This is my home, you'll be safe here." He told the terrified girls. "Can y'all please tell me where AlaHanDrea went?"

"She went to look for Danalli. She looked worried," the oldest of the 3 told him.

Braynar decided it was best to go ahead and shift, to calm the girls down a bit.

They were shocked to see him shift.

"See? Dragons are people, too!" He chuckled.

"Please, what's your name, pretty girl?"

"Teresa. I'm called Teresa and this is Jan. The baby is Camile."

"Well, it's very nice to know you, Teresa."

"Wow, you are really a handsome guy! And so big and strong!"

"Well, thank you, Teresa.

Please relax... no one's going to hurt you, not with me around, they aren't.

I have an idea, would you care to dance?" He snapped his fingers & turned the music on.

Amazed by his magic, she smiled at him the prettiest smile, melting his heart a little...

"Dance? Uh, sure! O.k.," she agreed, nervously.

Braynar took her in his arms, gazed deeply into her eyes for a moment, then twirled her before pulling her back to him, then floating effortlessly around the dance floor, with her feet barely touching the floor, he made her feel like she was a princess at the ball!

"Wow! Braynar, you can really dance!

Say, Why do you wear a crown?"

"Because I'm Prince Braynar Saint George, Heir to the throne of Drakania."

"Oh wow!

Wow!

You're the future king of the world?"

"I am."

"I'm blessed!

I'm so blessed!

Thank you for rescuing us, your highness, as well as having us in your home."

"You're quite welcome, sweet lady. So, is the baby yours?"

"She's mine to take care of. Please excuse my boldness, your highness, but, I'm.. I'm ... Uh, I'm ....I'm... still a virgin." She told him, blushing.

Braynar got an instant erection when she said that.

"Pardon me for saying so, but aren't you a little old to still be a virgin?"

"Not really, not for a human."

"Have you been prepared yet?"

"Prepared? I'm not sure I know what you mean."

"Dragon females are prepared before their virginity is taken. The hymen is surgically removed. Afterwards, the females use dilators to gradually open themselves, so that their first experience is a pleasant one." He explained.

"Really? Oh, how cool is that?"

"I'm certified in virgins," Braynar boasted. "I do the removal procedure for girls.... When they are ready, that is. It's against our laws to take a virgin who has not been properly opened.

You see, the hymen is removed, because, the male penis is not to come in contact with female blood. Ever."

"Wow. Well, that makes perfect sense.

So, do girls come to you for their first time?"

"They do...."

"Wow! Everything I've been told about dragons is a lie!

I can't believe we can speak so openly about such a sensitive subject as this. Thank you for being so open and honest with me.

Where I'm from, it's highly improper for a young lady to speak so frankly with a man, so, my deepest apologies, if I crossed the lines speaking with you.

I don't mean to speak of forbidden subjects so bluntly, I sure hope that I didn't offend you, or give you the wrong idea."

"This is not a forbidden subject among dragons. It is a necessary subject to be discussed, especially when a male and female are interested in being with one another... such as... well.... speaking for me, you and I..." he explained.

Teresa blushed a very deep red.

"I love your deep bass voice. I could listen to you speak all the time..."

"Would you like to sing with me?" He asked.

"May I listen to you first?"

"If you'd like, I'll sing ya a song."

"Oh, Prince Braynar, I would love nothing more than for you to sing a song for me," she told the very large, handsome prince...

Much to her amazement,

Braynar used his magic & produced a piano, sat down and began playing, then began singing...

"It's in the air tonight... Oh can't you feel it........ it's in the air tonight...... I can feel it, it's in the air tonight... I saw you standing there

...so pretty......

so sexy .... so pure... ......I saw you standing there .... So beautiful...

So pretty.......

I saw you standing there.. I took you in my arms, floating across that floor.... And I can feel it in the air tonight..... I can feel it in the air tonight...... I long to touch.... your lips.....with mine... I long to taste......... your kiss...... And I feel it in the air tonight, oh, I feel it in the air tonight......

I want to be your....... Mr right.... I long to be your........ Mr Right... I need to be your........ Mr Right.......... Oh, I can feel it..... in ....the air tonight...

I would.... Never ..... hurt you.... I would........ never...... break your heart... I would......... Never....... hurt you...... I can feel it..... Feel it in the air tonight....

I can feel it in the air tonight.......................

Ladedadadedade.ladadadadedaaaa.... I can feel it in the air....... To .....night....."

Teresa sang the chorus with him. Their voices blended beautifully.

She sat next to Braynar on his piano bench...then began playing together with him, so, he scooched down and took the lower keys...... Surrendering half of the piano...

Much to Braynar's surprise, Teresa was quite an accomplished player, her own self...

Braynar just smiled real big, picked up the tempo and they both cut loose... doing some serious pounding of the ivory! They were both having so much fun, they hadn't noticed Jan and Camile were up dancing away to the music...

When the song ended, Braynar turned towards her, took her face in his strong hands and kissed her ever so sweetly...

The kids were giggling in the background...

Electricity shot through Teresa like nothing she'd ever felt before!

She melted in his arms! Completely submissive....

He put his arms around her, kissing her with passion, igniting a fire deep inside of her.

The next thing she knew, she was coming to in another room, dimly lit, on a table, near a fireplace... She was wearing nothing but a white gown, with blankets tucked around her.

"Well, hello there, Sleeping Beauty!" Braynar said to her. "Everything went just fine.

The procedure went very smoothly. I performed a Hymonectomy for you. We rarely say anything before the procedure, because we need you calm when you're put to sleep.

How do you feel?"

"Fine. So, I'm not a virgin anymore?".

"Oh, no, sweetheart, you're still a virgin! You will remain a virgin until you decide not to be.

All I did was to remove that pesky piece of skin, that has to be ripped apart in order for you to have sex, because, That's very painful.

I used instruments to reach it, nothing flesh has entered you. So now, when you decide it's time, there is nothing to rip apart."

"What an incredible gift you have given me! I don't know quite what to say.

Oh my, you've seen me naked... way naked... You've seen my everything ." She giggled.

"Braynar, you've given me such an awesome gift! I honestly don't know what to say."

"Say you feel it, too.

Tell me I'm not the only one who feels this way... Look at me, tell me if you feel it too... " He said, then leaned down and kissed her again, pulling her close ... He could tell from her breathing that she was more than ready...

He backed off a little.

Teresa, I need to talk to you for a minute."

"O.k. you sound so serious!"

"Because what I have to say Is serious.

What I feel is real. Now, if you're with me, then you're with Me.

However, I, I am a Prince and the future ruler of the world.

I have women.

More than one.

I love them all very much.

I will have more in the future.

My ladies are well cared for...

Now, If you're My lady, then you're MY lady.

Do you understand that?

Other women do not mean I feel less for you.

What I have with you is different than what I have with the others.

What you and I have is real....

Really real.

Electric...

And...I'm already falling in love with you, Teresa...

I'm just being straight with you.

I never want to break your heart. Nor do I want my heart to be broken.

Now, AlaHanDrea is a subject all by herself. I'm deeply in love with her and am fiercely loyal to her.

We are about to become parents together.

Still, she is with who she wants to be with, when she wants to be with them. She loves many, like me, she is allowed, she is a queen.

Marry me and you will be a queen, but a different kind of a queen than AlaHanDrea or Isabel.

They are born Queens...

Both are warrior Queens.

They lead the army's in battle...

Both are victorious without question.

Together, they are an unstoppable force!

The warriors of Taurus 9 are the best there is in the known universe, so says the watchers, and, they should know!

Those two females keep the world safe for the rest of us.

Together with Bob, the world is a safer place to live.

So, AlaHanDrea plays by AlaHanDrea's Rules...

"Your highness, Prince Braynar, Am ... Am I allowed to fall in love with you? I mean, for real...?" She asked, with stars in her eyes...

"Oh, sweet baby girl, yes... Please yes......" He said as he kissed her again...

He touched her in ways she had never dreamed of being touched... It was obvious he was very educated in the art of pleasing females...

She hoped beyond hope that this was really real... And not just some game a royal was playing...

Anything that man wanted from her, she was prepared to give to him!

She suddenly wanted him more than she wanted air to breath! She didn't care in that moment whether it was going to be just the once, or, become a common thing, but either way, she was good. She couldn't think of a better way to lose her virginity ...

What a story to tell when she's much older!

He asked her several times if she was sure, if she was really sure...

All she could do was beg him, saying, "oh yes, oh please yes......!"

He felt compelled to warn her, "Teresa, we might make a baby, we could very easily make a baby!"

"O.k. if that happens, then, I will have your baby," she said, looking in his eyes, seeing sincerity...

He kissed her with even more passion then before, then stopped again.

"I don't want to push you into something you're not really ready for. You do remember, I'm a dragon, right? A giant, Man Eating, Fire Breathing, Dragon of epic proportions. I'm the largest of all of the dragons!

And as royal as royal can be."

"You, sir, are not a dragon, you are a Magnificent Dragon Prince!

But my question is, are you a man that shifts into a dragon, or a dragon that shifts into a man?"

"Does it matter?

First and foremost, I am a Dragon.

Actually, that's not completely true.

I'm half Dragon."

"Half Dragon?"

"My father is King Raynar, of the Watchers, heir to the throne of the Watchers. Which, makes me heir to 2 thrones...one that sits over Taurus 9, the other sits over billions of worlds all across the vastness of space.... Sitting in judgement of all species, everywhere."

"Oh, oh wow!

Seriously?

Well ya, Braynar, Raynar, Boy Raynar is Braynar, I get it now.... But, I thought King George is your father?"

"It's a long story, nows not really the time..."

"You're going to be a magnificent king, no matter which throne chooses you first, ... "

she said rather prophetically...

Braynar suddenly felt as if the weight of the world was lifted from his strong shoulders! It was the way she worded it. All that time he was thinking he'd be forced to choose between thrones one day, when it would be the throne that chooses him.... He worried for nothing!

"Woman, please hear my words I'm saying to you...

I am honestly falling deeply in love with you...

You just lifted a tremendous weight off my shoulders!

Thank you so much! Thank you so, so much!

You're right, when the time comes, the throne will choose me... And hopefully, you will sit next to me, on your own throne... As a queen...a beautiful and desirable, queen...." Braynar told Teresa.

"What woman could resist you, Prince Braynar?

I mean, just look at you, Bray!

Baby, your muscles have muscles!

You are absolutely gorgeous inside and out....your voice is incredible, Bray, you are the whole package, plus, darlin!

I've never been more sure of anything in my entire life... Thank you so much for choosing me, Bray,

and...

I Love your hair!"

"Thank you, sweet love...." Bray commented...

"Ya know, I can think of no sweeter gift than the one you're giving me with such a positive, absolutely incredible, fairy tale, first experience...

"Now, c'mere, big boy, I've got something special for you, your highness... Just for you..." She said, as she was unlacing her top, letting the girls out...

"Braynar fought the urge to giggle at her, trying to act all vixen... A virgin trying to be a vixen was a bit humorous, but still sexy! He couldn't

believe the reaction he was having to sweet innocence being like that...
He was sure he was going too love keeping this one as a pet...

uh....

Queen.....

A lesser queen, but, still a Queen.....

AKA Property of the crown...

Tears were streaming down her cheeks. She had never imagined in her wildest dreams that she'd ever be a queen! Yet, here she was, with the future king of the world!

If she didn't know better, she'd think Prince Braynar was asking her to become his wife!

But, she'd only known him for 2 days! Well, known of him one day and known him one day . She thought for sure she'd heard him wrong.

"Braynar, this is all so unreal, yet so very real! I want to belong to you and only to you.

And Braynar, I want you!

I want to feel you... I want to know you.... Know how you feel!

I've never felt a man before, and I want to feel you!

All of you!

May I please see all of you?

Touch all of you???

I've never seen a man, not all of him, before."

"You've never even seen a naked man?"

"No, I haven't,"

"Baby girl, you can touch any part of me you want to touch! Feel free to explore me all you want!"

"What's this?" She asked, patting his pouch .

"It's my egg pouch."

"Your what?"

"My egg pouch. Female dragons lay eggs. Male dragons carry those eggs in our pouches until they hatch," he explained.

"So, you're pregnant!"

"I suppose you could say that and not be completely wrong... " He told her.

He gasped when her hand found him.

"Wow! You're a big man!,"

"Don't worry, you will open up for me, here, let me show you," he said with a naughty smile.

They laid in each other's arms, breathless, chatting about different things he did to and for her. She was so curious!

He was answering her many questions as best he could...

Braynar was doing his best to make sure she always felt good about her first time.

The last thing he wanted to do, was to make her feel used, or bad in any way.

"We need to go check on the kids. I can hear rain falling, sounds like its raining really hard," Braynar told Teresa.

Reluctantly, they both got up and got dressed.

Braynar went over, took her in arms again, tilted her face up to look at him, and said, "I really do love you, Teresa. I'm looking forward to this love growing ever stronger," then he kissed her again, making her knees go weak...

"Braynar, I'm not happy about our village men being massacred... Please know that I'm in no way happy about any of that, but, that happening brought me to you and I'm so grateful to have something so wonderful come outta something so terrible!

The man that paid my bride price, actually tried to save his own Hyde by offering me up to those men. They killed him and took me anyway.

Those men put Jan and Camile in the same cage with me and told me I was to take care of them."

"Do you know what happened to the babies mother?"

"I think they killed her. They made a big deal about killing women that resisted, so the rest of us would behave.

They made us watch while they slit women's throats, stabbed them repeatedly, then left them to lay and bleed to death.

Other women got their necks broken. They took a sword and cut a couple of ladies in half. They hung others by their feet and left them to die a slow deaths.

Their cruelty was enough to make the rest of us do as we were told.

They lined most of the men up in groups and shot them dead, after making them watch the women being murdered.

They even killed a bunch of kids just to show that they would." She told him, obvious disgust in her voice.

"You know those men live still. They are in my food pits." Braynar told her.

"You're going to eat them, aren't you?"

"I am.

Very slowly and painfully. They will feel agony beyond what they did to others...

Does it bother you that I eat humans?"

"I would be a liar if I said it didn't bother me a little... Given that I'm human and all, but, I've always heard that y'all basically only eat the worst of the sinners... Is that true?"

"It is."

"I also eat meat. Not humans, of course, but I am a carnivore... I enjoy eating meat. Of course, I cook mine first and it's usually already dead and cut up... So, who am I to pass judgement?

You keep the crime rate low, that's a great contribution..."

"I do not feel sorry for the food. They choose a seat on my table.... They already know that sin makes them stink ... Such a luscious stink it is, to... Makes me hungry just thinking about it...

Not like their food.

They eat whoever, whatever, they run across when they are hungry... No offense...."

"Bray, baby, listen to that storm out there! What's that loud noise?"

"Hail is falling from the sky! We'd better get back to the kids. C'mon..."

None of them had ever been in a super cell storm before. The funnels dropping all around the edge of the giant vortex in the sky, were leaving a wide path of destruction in their wake.

Fortunately, Braynar and his new human girls, were deep inside of the mountain, safe from the horrid tornados and their horrific trail of destruction`.

Braynar was carrying Jan & the baby. The girls felt very safe, with Prince Braynar.

Jan was actually riding on his shoulder, while the baby sat on his neck, behind his head.

Teresa loved the way this giant of a man, was treating the young girls so tenderly and protectively.

Male dragons were very nurturing creatures by nature.

Braynar flicked his hand & the music began to play, with Jan and Camile still riding on his neck & shoulder, he took Teresa's hand, twirled her, then pulled her back up against his chest, stared deeply into her eyes, then began dancing all of them around the floor, as high winds, hail the size of a fist, thunder, lightning and a variety of types of tornados, along with flash flooding, causing mud & rock slides all around them, continued...

The inhabitants of Taurus 9 had no idea what severe weather was before that storm defined it for them.

But, inside of that mountain, 3 girls were feeling safe and loved, in, of all places, a Dragons Lair!

Chapter 6

AlaHanDrea was in absolute awe of the power contained in the super cell storm! She was determined to find out how to harness, then absorb the storms energy...

The vortexes we hypnotic to her. Dangerously hypnotic!

Worrying over Danalli, was probably the only thing strong enough to break the vortex spell.

AlaHanDrea hated volcanic mountains... Cooled lava flows blocked magic, due to the ore they contained. `

The teen queen screamed when she saw where the entrance to Danalli's lair used to be.

Blasting through cooled lava was no easy task! There HAD to be another way into his place!

As long as AlaHanDrea had lived just outside of that mountain, she never ventured through the labyrinth of corridors running throughout... connecting all of the dragons lair's that called that particular mountain home.

Exploring the mountains never did appeal to her. She wasn't one to enjoy having her powers restricted.

AlaHanDrea sat down, concentrating on Danalli so hard, the entire flock heard her cries...

She HAD to find him! One way or another, she had to find him!

She felt them before she saw them... King Neptune and Dane!

Dane was holding a Trident of his own, looking very much like the young God of the Seas...

AlaHanDrea ran over to roll herself up in King Neptune hair, when he blocked her and had her connect with Dane instead.

He looked sexier every time she saw him. She had to admit, he looked incredible as a young man, early in his 20's

Once the connection was made, power serged through Dane like nothing he'd ever felt before!

Dane pointed his Trident at the rock wall and began blasting away at the Cooled Lava flow that was now blocking the entrance to Danalli's lair.

AlaHanDrea separated herself, becoming 2, then shrank the new her, as tiny as she could get, rushing to search all of the blast spots, looking for even a pin hole she could fit herself through.

Dane finally made her stop, after almost blasting her 3 times in a row...

He told her to save her energy and just wait a minute... he'd focus all of their power on one spot until a hole was created.

Dane stood in one spot, while his father stood on the other side of the same wall, then began firing everything they had towards blasting that cooled lava, turned hard iron.

King Neptune, Dane and AlaHanDrea all three, all of a sudden felt stronger... They turned to look... They could hardly believe their eyes, they saw George, Raynar, Mr. Jax, Healix, Isabel, Keithen, Braynar, Leon, Bjorn, William, Johan, JayDe, Kenneth, Brian, Paulio, Franklon, Craigen and the list went on...

Everyone began combining power until they had a laser beam coming from those tridents, hot enough to cut through that solid iron of a cooled lava flow.

Danalli was, after all, one of the heirs to the throne!

Once the laser cut through, water began pouring out from the hole! The caves were flooded! Fortunately, dragons were amphibious! There was no way for anyone to go through that hole. Not with water pouring out of it like that.

Then it hit AlaHanDrea like a ton of bricks!

Teresa, Jan and the baby weren't amphibious!

AlaHanDrea screamed, "Teresa!"

Braynar shot out of there like he was fired from a rocket!

AlaHanDrea was hot on his trail!

Both of their hearts stopped for a moment when they saw the results of a massive land slide covering up where the entrance to Braynar's Lair used to be!

"Teresa!" AlaHanDrea screamed, as she began blasting and blasting at the tons of rock and debris...

The Bonner sisters appeared, very much in dragon state. They began helping to move the tons and tons of endless debris. The more stuff they'd move, the more that came tumbling down to replace it...it seemed as tho they were moving backwards, trying to reach the girls.... AlaHanDrea finally began blasting at the side of the mountain attempting to blow a new hole into the side of that mountain!

She couldn't join with Braynar, because most of her was still back looking for Danalli.

The Bonner sisters shocked Braynar and AlaHanDrea, when they combined to create one big beast!

"Now THAT'S a neat trick!" AlaHanDrea exclaimed!

The newly formed creature then joined with Braynar to create one hell of a super being!

Together, they blasted through rock, metals, dirt... Finally beginning to punch holes into the side of that mountain, releasing tons and tons of water....

Paralyzing Fear gripped the hearts of everyone there...

Suddenly, AlaHanDrea vanished. Braynar didn't have time to worry about how or why, he had to reach his girls and fast!

He tore at the side of that mountain like nothing ever seen before! The combined strength of the Bonner sisters, added to his own strength, was enough to make him into a super sized bull dozer, chomping away at that mountain side until a hole the size of a large tank, allowed the water to flow out , effectively draining the flooded caverns.

Braynar didn't have to look very long before he found the girls, drowned, laying across boulders. The Bonner sisters separated from Braynar as well as each other, shifting back to human state.

They all began attempting to resuscitate the girls, blowing air into their water soaked lungs, pumping on their chests, begging them to breath.

Braynar hadn't meant to leave them alone, but he heard the distress calls about his brother...

Guilt washed over him as he continued attempting to bring Teresa back, but not being successful.

The Bonner sisters finally laid Jan and the baby down, tears rolling down their faces. Their efforts were of no use. Jan and the baby weren't responding to their efforts to revive them. There was no sign of life!

Braynar screamed for them to not stop, so, even tho they felt it was useless, they went back to trying to resuscitate the girls.

Much to the sisters surprise, the baby coughed, then threw up a bunch of water, coughing, spitting and crying!

Everyone tried even harder on Jan. They worked on her and worked on her, finally holding her upside down by her feet, pounding on her back, until the water all drained out of her lungs...

"Mitchin!" Braynar called out.

"Braynar, what happened? Oh my! Give her here!" Mitchin said, as he took Jans body, breathing life back into her until she began to cough.

Braynar was holding Teresa's lifeless body, tightly in his arms, rocking gently, crying and singing to her, tears flowing like a river.

Mitchin went over to him and took Teresa from him.

The confident angel held her in his arms. It looked like he was giving her a big ol kiss...

Moments later, Teresa opened her eyes.

She was startled to see herself in the arms of a handsome stranger.

The last thing she remembered was trying to tread water as the caverns quickly filled up with sea water, praying that Braynar would come back and save them...

Mitchin looked in her eyes and that time, it was a kiss. Braynar ran over to her, took her from Mitchin, hugging her tightly and thanking Mitchin over and over again for bringing her back to life.

Braynar had Jan and the baby in his arms as well, hugging all three, relieved to have them all alive....

Mitchin went over to him and took Teresa back from him, then vanished.

"Mitchin, what the???? Where'd he go?

Mitchin!" He called out, finally deciding that Mitchin must have been needing to fix something with Teresa, So, he tried to relax and focussed on Jan and the baby.

After all, Mitchin was an angel... Teresa was safe with an Angel....

Teresa didn't know what to think! She came to in this man's arms, Braynar took her, then this man took her back!

He had not said a single word to her yet. He just looked in her eyes with so much love, then kissed her again.

Nothing in the world existed or mattered while he kissed her.

She had never felt that way before! It was incredible!

She found herself becoming lost in that kiss... It was as if she were floating through a dream!

This man, who ever he was, had brought her back to life.

Teresa was fully aware of how close she had become to staying dead... had it not been for this incredible man... now kissing her with love and passion...

The next thing she new, this man was pleasuring her like nothing she had ever felt before...

She didn't even try to object to anything that he was doing to her...

It was happening, so, she was determined to enjoy every second of it.

They made love for hours on end, never saying a single word to one another.

She fell into a deep sleep, laying in his arms.

When she woke up, she was laying in a super soft bed with big fluffy pillows and a soft, fluffy blanket. A fire was crackling in the fireplace, music was playing softly and a cold glass of juice sat on small table by the bed.

Teresa had no idea where she was or who had her... she even questioned what was real and what was not.

One of the most handsome men she had ever seen in her entire life walked into the room. Her memory came flooding back. She smiled, realizing that was the man she had made love to.

"Well, hello there, sleepy head, I was beginning to get a little worried about you, how are you feeling?"

Mitchin asked her.

"Fine, I suppose. Just a little confused, I guess. Thank you for bringing me back to life. I didn't much care for being dead."

"You're quite welcome," he said, as he sat down beside her on the bed.

"May I please ask, who are you? I mean, besides my hero..."

"Ya, kind of rude of me to make love to you before I introduced myself." He chuckled.

"I'm your new owner. I took you from the dragon. He let you die. I made you live. You're mine, now."

"I am? Cool!" She said, with a big smile.

"Yes, you are. It's the law. I brought you back from the clutches of certain death, you now belong to me."

"Well, that's great!"

"You'd probably rather be mine than a dragons, anyway. Even if that dragon is the Future king of the world. I trump his king of the world..."

"You do? Wow! Incredible!"

"Yes, I do! He could never out rank me. Not even if he lived 1000 lifetimes, could he ever outrank me.

He is a beast. I am not."

"You're human?"

"Oh, Heavens No."

"O.k. well, if you're not human and you're not a beast... What are you?"

He bent down and kissed her, sending waves of electricity surging through her whole being.

"Does it really matter?"

"No, I suppose not. Do you shift into another human looking being, or creature being???"

"No, I don't. I do have wings, tho," he said, then flexed his back muscles to produce his wings.

"Oh! Wow! They are Magnificent! You're gorgeous!"

"Thank you, did you hear somebody calling out?" Mitchin asked.

"Mitchin! Hey Mitchin, you around, buddy?" Keithen called out.

"If you will excuse me for a moment..."

"Oh wow, he's named after a famous Angel!" Teresa said out loud to herself.

She could hear some of what Mitchin and Keithen were talking about...

"But it's y'all's own laws that make her mine! She wasn't facing certain death, she was full on, all of the way drowned, dead! I did what none of you could do, I brought her back to life, she belongs to me!"

"Dude, man, but, you're an Angel!"

"Correction, I'm a vacationing Angel-and I don't see anywhere that the law makes an exception and disqualifies angels! The girl belongs to me, Keithen! Go ask your father, he will tell you... the girl is mine, according to your own laws!""

"My brother loves her."

"Your brother will get over it!

The girl is mine.

Look, I left 2 of them with him and only took the one. Tell him that I said to quit trying to be greedy, he knows the law."

"Of course he does and you're right, Mitchin. The girl IS yours. Legally, morally, the girl now belongs to you. Thank you for leaving the other 2."

"Your welcome. Please tell your brother that I'm sorry she passed away.

I didn't have to bring her back. I brought her back because I looked at her and I wanted her to be alive and be with me! I HAD to make her live again! I know I'm right about her, Keithen. She's mine and I need her.

As much as I love Athena, I need one that's all mine and no one else's.

This one belongs to me. Tell your brother that I said that if he truly loves her, he'll be happy that she is no longer dead and that she's safe, living with a vacationing Angel.... Tell him to be happy for her...."

"You're perfectly right, Mitchin, and yes, I'll tell him what you said." Keithen told him as he was preparing to leave.

"My God! He is not only an Angel of God, he is the Angel, Mitchin!" She said out loud to herself. I got brought back to life by the angel, Mitchin! I made love to an arc angel! I didn't know angels could have sex!"

"We can't, normally. I'm on vacation. I can have all of the sex I want to have," Mitchin explained. "vacations don't happen very often." He climbed back up on the bed, all playful like....

Teresa smiled real big... you're an angel! A real, live, honest to goodness, angel! And not just any ol angel, you're Mitchin, the arc angel!"

"Temporarily in the flesh!" He said, bowing to her.

"I'm with an angel! How long are you on vacation for?"

"Only a couple of ..... hundred years or so.... " he teased.

"That's why you said you trump his king of the world! Oh wow! You talk to God! You know God first hand!"

"Ya, but it's not like I can just go up to Him any ol time I feel like it...."

"Maybe not, but you can go see Him and talk to Him! Wow! Braynar is not happy that you took me, is he?"

"He'll get over it. Now, c'mere, you!" He said, grabbing her by the ankles and pulling her across the bed to him. He, leaned over her and kissed her with deep passion.

She was once again lost in that kiss! She decided that if a lady hadn't been kissed by an Angel, she hadn't been properly kissed!!! He took her to places she'd NEVER been before!

A couple of hours passed.

As they lay catching their breath, she asked him, "o.k. I get it that I belong to you. Am I like your wife?"

"That's a very good question, actually. You're more like my queen. You are mine. A wife would be my equal, you're human... you are my Queen."

"Oh wow, you can make me a queen?" Teresa asked, surprised.

"Of course I can, I'm an Angel... you, are Queen Teresa. Her Royal Majesty, Queen Teresa."

He reached behind his back and pulled a tall, round box out... handing it to her to open.

"For me?" She squealed.

"Go ahead, open it!"

"Oh Mitchin, it's gorgeous! It's incredible! It's mine? Oh look! It says Teresa on it! Oh, Mitchin! I love it!"

"Here, let me help you put it on... there, now, you are my Queen, officially," he said, then laid her backwards on the bed, kissing her with passion....

Round 3.....

They were barely catching their breath when Mitchin heard AlaHanDrea calling desperately for help! She must have found Danalli!

"Sweetheart, I have to go! AlaHanDrea needs me! I'll be back. Please stay here and don't go anywhere. I won't be very long..." he said, then kissed her and took off!

"Gee, I wish I had a sandwich," she said out loud to herself. Much to her surprise, a sandwich appeared. She was startled to say the least.

"O.k, now that was weird!" She said out loud to nobody. She said she wished she had some cool-aid to go with it, and sure enough, a pitcher of cool-aid and a glass appeared on a floating tray. She squealed with excitement.

"I can do magic! Oh wow! I can do magic! She made scuba gills and foot fins appear, then squealed some more! (Scuba gills were a contraption that retrieved oxygen from the water, much smaller and easier to carry than oxygen tanks and they never ran out of oxygen, like tanks do)

The anxiety over being in a cave left her when the gills appeared.

"I can do magic! I belong to the arc angel, Mitchin, I'm his Queen, and I can do magic!" She said out loud to herself.

She felt badly for Braynar, but he did leave her to drown. At least Mitchin didn't bring the children for her to have to care for. Still, she was going to miss Braynar.

Braynar was real to her. He didn't act all superior, even tho he really was... He behaved genuinely jend very romantically.

Still, what Mitchin did was hot! That handsome stranger brought her back to life, snatched her out of Braynar's arms, took her home with him and made crazy love to her, silently...

Her new life was going to take some getting used to and first things first, she had a few things to say to God... Most importantly, thank you.

"Braynar!" She exclaimed. "What are you doing here? Mitchin went to see AlaHanDrea for something."

"I'm not here to see Mitchin. I'm here to see you!"

"I don't want to cause trouble for you!" Teresa replied.

"Look me in my eyes and tell me that you don't love me and I will leave right now..."

"I can't do that, Braynar. I can't do that!"

Chapter 7

Relief flooded AlaHanDrea when she finally saw Danalli through a tiny hole in the rocks. "We found him! We found him!" she screamed.

Dane and Neptune went running to her and began blasting with everything they had in them, until they managed to make a hole big enough to fit through.

AlaHanDrea squeezed through that hole and rushed over to Danalli, laying unconscious across a rock. He was in Dragon state.

Dane and his dad continued blasting until the hole was big enough for them as well.

AlaHanDrea crawled up on Danalli, laid her head against his chest and began checking for a heart beat. .. only, she wasn't finding one...

King Neptune picked her up by the waist and moved her out of the way. Dane grabbed ahold of her and took her to the other room to give his dad room to work.

"AlaHanDrea, calm your butt down!" Dane said firmly as he held her by the shoulders.

Unsure of what else to do, Dane bent down and kissed her.

She couldn't help herself, she melted in his arms!

Dane had grown into an amazing man!

No woman could resist him!

She was lost in that kiss... completely lost...

King Neptune waited a moment before telling her that he was successful in bringing Danalli back to life.

From the looks of things, Dane had everything in hand... he found a way to comfort her that worked....

"I've never stopped loving you, AlaHanDrea and I never will..."

He said, then kissed her again, before standing her back upright.

"I don't mean to disturb you two, but, I thought you might want to know, Danalli is alive again. However, I had to put him into a forced coma for now. He needs to heal. Healix is going to stay with him.

AlaHanDrea, does Danalli have eggs? Is he expecting?"

"Yes, he does. He has 3 of them, are they o.k.?"

"I honestly don't know. Why don't the two of you go someplace where you can get some rest, AlaHanDrea, we'll tend to Danalli. You're not doing anybody any good all worn out like you are, especially yourself. You look drained!"

"Ya, I could use some rest. I'm pretty worn out."

"I'll stay with you, AlaHanDrea." Dane volunteered...

"What about Dana?"

"I dunno, what ABOUT Dana? If I ask her, she will insist I stay with you. And I know Dana, she'd insist I ... uh.... Entertain you.... As well...."

"Well, we can't have you upsetting Dana... now, can we?" She asked, rather seductively.

"No, we sure can't. Wouldn't be polite..." Dane said, almost in a trance of desire....

Dane was right behind ALaHanDrea as she led him to a hut.... As soon as the door closed behind Dane, AlaHanDrea turned around coming almost nose to lower chest, with Dane.

"You've gotten very tall, there, now, boyfriend..."

"Ya, I've grown an inch or two.

You haven't..." he teased, then lifted her up off of her feet and onto a tall table to sit on, where he could look her in the eyes...

"Woman, I swear, you grow prettier with every passing day! I don't ever want to have to live in a world without you in it!" he told her, then kissed her with unbridled passion.

Dane had a way of making her forget about everything and everyone, focussing only on the two of them.

They were both overcome with desire! There love for one another was unbreakable.

The two of them couldn't resist being together. They meant no disrespect towards Danalli... there was just nothing either of them could do at the time, so, they focused on each other....

They barely had time to catch their breath before they had to throw some clothes on.

Both of them thought they heard king Neptune hollering about Danalli waking up....

When they opened the door to his room, they knew something was terribly wrong...

"Mitchin!!!" AlaHanDrea called out...

"Yes child, what's wrong?" Mitchin asked.

"It's Danalli, Mitchin, something is bad wrong!"

"Here, why don't the two of you go in the other room and leave me and King Neptune to see about this?" Mitchin told her.

Reluctantly, she agreed.

They didn't have to wait very long for Mitchin to come back out.

"AlaHanDrea, he lost the eggs. They were cracked open during the surge of flood water. It appears as tho the water slammed him against the boulders, shattering all 3 of the eggs. I'm so sorry. They were yours, weren't they?"

"She couldn't answer him for crying.

"I'm so sorry, baby girl! I'm so very sorry.

Danalli is hurt.

Being slammed against the boulders as hard as he was, has caused some internal damage.

A couple of his vital organs are badly damaged."

"What are you saying, Mitchin?"

"I'm saying that I don't know if Danalli is going to be able to pull through this one."

"Take that back! Take that back right now!" She yelled. "Mitchin, you take that back right now!" She screamed... She got up and went over to Danalli, shrank herself, then rolled up in his Mane.

Power surged through Danalli, causing his body to quake.

AlaHanDrea held on to Danalli, not allowing the power to make him grow giant, instead, harnessing all of the power and putting it towards healing....

King Neptune, Dane, Mitchin, Jax and Healix all stood watching in utter disbelief, as Danalli's body was visibly healing itself... there wasn't anything anybody could do about the babies...

After a while, Healix, Mitchin, Neptune, Dane and Jax all helped to unroll AlaHanDrea and made her stop. At the rate she was going, she was liable to drain herself to the point of her own death. As it was, she was so depleted, she couldn't stand up.

"You can't die, Danalli!

I forbid you to die!

Danalli!

I forbid you to die!

Do you hear me?

I forbid you to die!" She screamed....

"Danalli St George, I command you to live !!! Do you hear me Danalli?

I said LIVE!" And with that, she collapsed.

Dane caught her before she hit the ground. He carried her over and laid her down in bed. She was barely breathing.

"y'all just take care of Danalli, I've got AlaHanDrea. I know how to make her better..." Dane told them as he scooped her back up and carried her back to the hut...

He knew he had to generate as much power as he possibly could, so, he turned the music up loud and became very aggressive with her... Pinning her down in a show of pure dominance...

he ripped her clothes off, throwing them across the room.

Dane went after her as if he hadn't been with anyone in ages and his hunger was all consuming... she finally began to respond! He laid her sideways in the hammock and began giving her what she needed to heal...

There was nothing tender or easy that time. It couldn't be. He had to generate as much electricity as he possibly could and gentle just didn't do it..... He had to drive the passion thru the roof! So, he pulled out all the stops! Gave her the best he had to give... And it worked! After about an hour or so, She was fully energized! It wore him plum smooth out, but she was much better!

Neptune and Healix were amazed at how much healing had occurred from AlaHanDrea pushing power thru Danalli like she did...

From the sounds of things coming from the hut, Dane had her fully recharged!

Neptune, Jax, and Healix just looked at each other, shaking their heads and grinning from all of the sounds coming from the hut...

"Whatever works!" King Neptune Commented... They all chuckled at his comment.

When AlaHanDrea finally came back from the hut, a walk of all of about ten feet, Danalli was coming to. She didn't want to be the one to tell him about the eggs.

Raynar, Isabel and George showed up. Healix told them the sorrowful news before they went in to see Danalli...

George told everyone to please leave him and Barbara alone with their son for a bit. They wanted to be the ones to tell him what happened.

Braynar and Keithen were stunned when they heard the news.

Neither of them had announced about their eggs and decided they weren't going to, either. Both of them put their eggs away for safe keeping. Without body warmth, the eggs lay dormant...

Both decided it was best not to even say a word about it... Both of them a bit relieved that they wouldn't be becoming father's right away... Some day, when they were both ready...

Both brothers worried for their other brother.

He was so proud of his eggs...

They knew he would always grieve for them.

Both of them knew that Danalli would need to become a father before either of them could bring their eggs to hatch ... A father to AlaHanDrea's eggs...

They all heard Danalli scream when his parents told him the news.

Tears streaked down everyone's faces... As AlaHanDrea passed out, Dane caught her, cradled her and began singing to her.

She had just lost her first 3 offspring and it was beginning to sink in...

Dana popped up, said she felt them ... She sat next to Dane, with her arms around him, gently rocking with him and AlaHanDrea.

Dana began softly singing along with Dane.

Much to everyone's surprise, Danalli got up off of the table, shook himself off and shifted to man state, then walked over and took AlaHanDrea out of Dane and Danas arms, then vanished with her.

No one tried to follow them.

He and AlaHanDrea used their combined magic to retrieve their crushed eggs. They went over them, then gave them a proper burial. They fell asleep in each other's arms, laying on top of the grave.

They found themselves in the field of flowers, the same place they had been together when they cheated death. They knew in an instant why they were there.

A few moments passed, then 3 people came walking up, 2 boys and a girl ...

"Mom, dad, hello. Please don't be sad. You can try again! And we'll, us three, will come back! It will be us... We promise! The only thing you really lost was the bodies that were meant to be ours, so, make new ones! But, not right this second, please take time for daddy to heal first.

We are not lost, we are simply postponed. It's okay to be disappointed, but grieve not, because we aren't lost.

They sat and comforted their parents before leaving, so Danalli and AlaHanDrea could wake up and be better.

They woke up, embracing each other, wiping each other's tears away and smiling at one another.

"We've got some pretty incredible kids, baby girl," Danalli told her.

"Yes, we sure do," she agreed. "They'll be o.k waiting among the flowers, just not for too awfully long..." AlaHanDrea told him.

They spent a couple of days, relaxing, talking, just being together.

But AlaHanDrea had to know, so, she called Mitchin.

"Jan and the baby live. Teresa died.

She drowned.

I made her live again. She's mine now." Mitchin declared.

"But, what about Braynar?" AlaHanDrea asked him.

"What about Braynar? He let her die! I didn't Have to make her live again! I could have left her dead! But, I chose to break the rules and make her live again and she's MINE!" Mitchin declared.

AlaHanDrea couldn't help but to notice the changes in Mitchin, that being flesh was making in him.

She hoped and prayed he wouldn't become lost...

Chapter 8

"Wow! We made it! Can you believe it? We actually made it! We're in Drakonia!" Jenn said to her daughter, Teri.

"Ya, but Drakonia is a big place, how are we going to find her?" Teri asked her mother.

"That, I really don't know. She was coming here to see her son. I'm not sure why he came here, not being raised among humans like he was.

To tell you the truth, I don't care if I never see Danalli again!

He should have told me!

But, Barbara, well, she has a right to know that you are her granddaughter.

I should have told her ages ago.

Danalli could have at least told me the truth about what he is... He should have told me the truth!"

"You're Angry that I'm part dragon, aren't you?"

"Oh, no, sweetheart, I love you just as you are!

I promise you!

But Danalli should have told me he is at least half dragon!"

"Maybe I should try to call him, If I call him, maybe he will hear me, mother."

"Then go ahead, call him..." She said, reluctantly.

Moments later, a startled Danalli appeared.

"Jenn!

Wow!

What a surprise!

It's been way too long! What brings you all of the way to Drakonia? How did you manage to summon me?" Danalli asked.

"I'm actually looking for your mother," Jenn told him.

"My Mother? O.K.

Oh, how rude of me, hello there, my name is Prince Danalli, and who might you be?"

"My name is Teri. You're a prince? Does that make me a princess?" Teri asked him.

The look of confusion on Danalli's face made them both giggle.

"You're my daddy, Prince Danalli."

"I am?"

"You are." She told him, smiling.

"You're beautiful!

I mean, look at you! You're beautiful!

I had no idea!

Why didn't I know before now?" He asked.

"I wasn't going to tell you at all. But then, I had a dream. In the dream, I think it may have been a wizard, came to see me and told me to come see your mother right away... and for me to tell her the truth.

So, here we are."

"Yes, here you are!

Wow...

I mean, wow! Jenn!

Well, c'mon, let's go see my mother!

You won't recognize my mother!

She's changed!

I take it that you already figured out that I'm a dragon..." Danalli shifted to dragon. Jenn and Teri stood in Awe of Danalli as a Dragon! He had them both get on his neck and flew them to go see the parents.

They landed a little bit of a walk away from the royal chambers.

"There's some stuff I need to tell you, Jenn. After mother got here, she found out that her missing husband was none other than King George! Ya, King George is my Father!"

"But, he's the King of the World!"

"Yes, I know."

"So, you're like, heir to the throne?"

"Yes.

I am.

One of three, actually.

He never even knew that mom was pregnant."

"Hmmm , it runs in the family," Jen commented.

"I'm so sorry, Jenn. I never meant to hurt you!

I was so sick of having to hide what I am. No matter how hard I tried to hide it, someone always found out and used it against me.

I didn't want to face you with my truth.

I chickened out... I love you so much, I don't think I could have withstood the rejection, so, I chickened out and just vanished.

Please, forgive me. I had no idea you were with child! Was she an egg or a live birth?"

"She was a live birth," Jenn answered, kinda mad like....

"That's incredible. She's incredible!" he picked Jenn up, held her tightly and spun her around telling her thank you, over and over again, then put her down and kissed her the kind of kiss that made her knees go weak.

Jenn never could stay angry at him, not after he kissed her, she couldn't.

Teri giggled at her parents kissing. It made them all three laugh. Danalli hugged them both.

"What's all the noise out here?" George asked as he stepped out from his chambers, followed by Barbara, Isabel and Raynar...

"Jenn! So good to see you, what are you and Teri doing all the way in Drakonia?" Barbara asked .

"Mom, you knew about Teri?" Danalli asked.

"What about Teri?"

"That she's my daughter," Danalli told her.

"She is? Teri, your my granddaughter? Why am I just now finding this out?" Barbara asked.

"The important thing, is that we know now, Mom," Danalli told her.

"You're so right, son. Welcome to the family, you two!"

"Jenn, Teri, this is King George, my father... His wife, Isabel...& Her husband, Raynar. Guys, this is my old girlfriend from back home and my daughter Teri... Excuse me, Princess Teri..."

"Cool! You're my grandpa? You're very handsome, your majesty. It's so nice to meet you all! So, Queen Isabel, are you also my grandma? Wait, I'm confused, is Raynar Isabel's Husband or is George her husband?"

"Yes, Raynar and George are her husband's... "

"Oh, very cool! I like that, very cool!" Teri said...

"And I am also George's wife," Barbara told her.

"I see you're expecting, congratulations!" Jenn told Barbara.

"Yes, that would be my fault," Raynar volunteered.

"So, your all 4 married to each other?" Jenn asked.

"Yes, we are... It wasn't planned this way, it worked out this way and we are all good with it... It works for us." Isabel said.

"O.k. so, I have 2 grandmas and 2 grandpas... I can live with that!" Teri told them.

"If y'all don't mind, I think we should have a party and introduce Teri to the kingdom," Danalli suggested.

"Of course, right away! How about this weekend?" George said.

Everyone was in agreement, so arrangements began being made.

The broadcast drones were all over that one! In hardly any time at all, everyone knew that a royal coming out ball was in the works!

AlaHanDrea rushed over to the royal chambers as soon as she heard about the ball.

She seemed excited to meet Danalli's old girlfriend and the child he never knew about.

Her and Teri hit it off right away. Jenn didn't quite know what to think about AlaHanDrea. She'd heard so many stories, she didn't know what to think.

She was positive they were close, she just wasn't sure how close.

The fairies went right to work making a home for the 2 new comers, per AlaHanDrea's request.

AlaHanDrea thoroughly warned Jen and Teri about the danger of the fairies.

The teen queen secretly hoped that Jenn and Teri would offer to help Braynar with his two girls. They were really keeping Braynar on his toes! Especially the baby!

The lions and bears were helpful, but they couldn't be expected to raise them for him.

They were his, plain and simple.

Teri fell in love with the baby.

Her and Jan filled a void in each others lives.

Being close to the same age made a huge difference. They both needed a best friend around close to their own ages.

They stayed up most of the night chit chatting. They actually got to sleep on the surface, since Jenn was there to watch them...

Danalli decided to give the girls a little space so they could get settled in.

Truthfully, he needed a little time to himself.

AlaHanDrea wasn't having it tho.

As soon as she got everyone settled, she wasted no time in going down to Danalli's lair. She couldn't find him, tho. It took a bit, but she finally found him in his lair at the top of the mountain.

She decided he no longer felt safe in his lower lair... and who could blame him, after everything he'd just been through!

"There you are!"

"Ya, here I are," he replied.

AlaHanDrea didn't say another word, she went over to him, sat down and put her arms around him trying to comfort him... Not an easy task...

And what timing for Jenn to show up with a child he never knew about... A child Jenn never told him about!

He knew she was upset at him for leaving, but to keep his child a secret? That was some serious stuff, there, now.

Of course, not telling her he was half dragon was pretty serious, also. Still, not mentioning his child... even to his mother...

AlaHanDrea just sat and listened while he fussed, hollered, griped, yelled and completely vented everything he was feeling inside.

Jenn's thoughts stayed on Danalli. She was feeling guilty now that she had seen him again.

She'd forgotten what a handsome man he really was. Of course, he was just a teen ager when she knew him before.

He had filled out quite nicely as a man!

Then there was the fact that he was the son of the king of the world!

And she was the mother of his child!

She suddenly found herself hoping and praying for Danalli's forgiveness!

All those years she spent angry at him, and there she was, hoping beyond hope that he would forgive her!

There had been no men after him.

Only him.

He was her first and he was her last!

They had finally done the deed and the next thing she knew, he was just gone!

She never knew why.

She had no idea that his secret was discovered... That a bully was threatening him with outing him to everyone, which, was what made him take off like he did.

All she knew, was that she gave in to their passion and then he was gone.

At first, she thought he left because she gave in...

Anger built... Then, when she discovered that she was pregnant... She all but lost it!

Raising Teri all lone had not been easy.

Then she had that dream...

That dream that told her to go find Barbara...

And Barbara! She looked half her age! And Pregnant!

At her age!

And!

She had wings!

Sleep was not coming easily for her.

"Psssst... Jenn, are you awake? It's me Braynar, Danalli's brother."

"Ya, come on in. Ya, I can't sleep," she admitted.

"I thought maybe. So, I decided to see if you'd like some company.

I'd like to talk to you, about Danalli."

"Is everything o.k?"

"No. Not really. That's what I want to discuss with you.

Danalli was in a bad accident just last week."

"Oh no! What happened?"

"Remember the big storms that blew through? Well, our caves flooded. The rushing water slammed Danalli hard against the boulders.

He was carrying 3 eggs in his pouch. All three were crushed.

Yes, male dragons have a pouch we carry eggs in... Momma lays them, we bring them to hatch...

All three of his were destroyed. Jenn, the flood waters did more than smash his eggs, they took his life!

AlaHanDrea wasn't having it!

King Neptune was there, helping to rescue him and managed to bring him back, but he wasn't going to survive his injuries, they were just too severe.

Our baby girl refused to allow him to die!

She combined power with him and focused on healing his body until it all but killed her!

She would have gladly died to save him.

Jenn, the eggs were hers and Danalli's eggs.

She was the mother.

They lost their children that day, she wasn't about to lose Danalli, too."

"And this just happened? And here I show up with the daughter I never told him about... Oh, what timing!

But! In my defense, I received a visit in my dreams telling me to come find Barbara and tell her the truth. So, I sold everything that Teri and I had and began our journey here."

"You did that based on a dream?"

"It was an intense dream."

"It must have been!"

"Danalli left right after the first time we made love together. He was gone for 3 months before I realized I was pregnant.

I should have told Barbara, but I didn't want Danalli to find out ...

Then, when Teri was born and I discovered she was a shape shifter... Well ......

Let's just say that I got very upset. Oh, don't get me wrong! I love Teri! It's just that he never told me! He should have told me..."

"We all make mistakes, Jenn.

All of us do.

I didn't find out that Raynar is my father until recently. And he didn't find out about me, either.

George had no idea that Danalli is actually his son, until we'd already known Danalli for years ...

We all make mistakes, Jenn.

But it does us no good to hold those mistakes against one another. We can't take back what is done.

We have to learn to accept, forgive and move on."

"Thank you, Braynar. You're very kind."

"So, what are you planning on wearing to the ball?"

"Oh, well, I hadn't really given it very much thought. Oh, it's a royal ball! I'll bet it's a formal one!"

"Don't stress. I have a few gifts for you. BTW, would you care for a glass of Nectar?"

"Oh, thank you, yes, I'd love one!"

Braynar used his magic to first produce a floating tray with nectar goblets, then a whole stack of gift boxes and 1 formal dress bag.

"Wow! I love how you do magic! That is so cool! Are all of those for me?"

"Just for you. Go ahead, open the dress first..."

"O.k, I'm so excited!"

She opened the bag and the look on her face almost made Braynar give a little chuckle...

"Oh! Braynar! This dress is magnificent!"

Braynar used his magic to change Jenn into the dress.

"Oh! Braynar! Oh wow!" She exclaimed.

"Go ahead, open the next one!" The proud prince instructed.

Silk shoulder gloves, crystal shoes, a gorgeous jeweled necklace with matching earrings, bracelets and rings... But it was the last box that almost made her faint ..

It was a crown!

"A crown? For me?"

"Yes, Princess Jenn, for you. Danalli is one of the future kings of the world and you gave him a child. You are a princess... And this is your crown. See, it even says Jenn right on it.... Here, let me help you put that on.... And the necklace, too. Wow! You look amazing!"

Braynar produced full length mirrors so she could see herself.

Tears began rolling down her cheeks when she saw herself.

Braynar made music start, then used his magic to produce a dance floor...

"Me lady, would you care to dance?" She turned back around to answer him and saw he was wearing a tuxedo! The nectar was making her feel giddy...

"I'd love to dance, thank you...." They stepped outside under the light of the moons and began dancing effortless around the floor... It was like being in a fairy tale!

They stopped for more nectar, then danced some more.

"Jenn, do you sing?"

"Braynar, everyone can sing, it's just that some really shouldn't. As a courtesy to others..." She laughed...

"Oh, I'd bet you have a nice voice!"

"Boy, you'd be losing that bet!" She teased... " However, had I a saxophone, then I could make some pretty noise..." Her drunk self boasted.

She no sooner said it then Braynar made it happen. A beautiful new saxophone with Jenn written on it's side!

She hadn't exaggerated, the girl could really play that horn!

The sound of the music attracted a few creatures with instruments of their own, which, attracted more creatures with instruments... Which attracted everybody... Pretty soon, a party was in full swing!

AlaHanDrea and Danalli heard the music and finally decided to go join the party. Danalli stopped before he was seen, hiding himself behind a bush for a moment, taking it all in. AlaHanDrea stopped with him for a bit.

"She's beautiful, Danalli."

"Yes, she is, isn't she."

"Go to her, Danalli. It's ok."

AlaHanDrea put his tux on him.

"Alright, alright, I'm going!" He said, then came out from behind the bush.

When Jenn put the sax down, she turned and saw him standing there.

She smiled. He held his hand out for her to take his hand and dance with him. She accepted his invitation.

"You look amazing, Jenn."

"Thank you. So do you!"

"So, Bray, what's a girl gotta do to get danced with around here?" AlaHanDrea asked.

"Would you care to dance with me?"

"I'd love to!"

Jenn was amazed at Braynar and AlaHanDrea dancing! Braynar motioned for Danalli, so, he excused himself for a moment and joined them. The three of them did some jaw dropping stunts, really showing off! Then, all of a sudden, a large dragon swooped down and snatched AlaHanDrea right out of the air! Braynar had thrown her up there thinking Danalli would catch her, and a dragon swooped down and grabbed her!

Braynar shifted and took to the skies! Danalli was right behind him! Several others shifted and took off after their Prince...

Things just got really real!

Jenn didn't know quite what to think!

Jan and Teri were quietly watching the dancing when it happened. They were really scared for AlaHanDrea. That's when they heard a male voice tell them to be afraid for the dragon, not AlaHanDrea.

"C'mon, you girls are going with me," the male voice said.

"Oh no we are not!" Teri said.

"Now look child, don't you be trying to give me a hard time. You come with me quietly and no one gets hurt."

"Get behind me, Jan!"

"Oh, you think you're some kind of a bad ass, eh, little girl?"

"Just go ahead and try it!" She told him. He lunged towards her and she blew a huge flame, engulfing him in flames! He ran, screaming, burning until he fell over dead!

Everyone came running to the girls. They quickly realized that grabbing AlaHanDrea was a distraction to get rid of all of the guards... It was an attempted kidnapping! Which meant, the man was not acting alone!

"Dang, Teri! That was cool! How'd you do that?" Jan asked her.

"Easy, I'm part dragon!" She said, then shifted.

She didn't look like any dragons anyone there had ever seen! Her body was shaped like a humans with wings and dragon skin. Her head was a cross between, with the facial features of a human, but the teeth of a dragon. She was actually quite beautiful.

Ooohs and aaahhhs rose up from the remaining crowd.

It was the first time Teri was ever able to shift and be proud!

Her smile lightened the mood for everyone.

"Teri, please stay in Dragon state! You are a very beautiful creature, please don't hide by shifting! Please, let everyone get a chance to see you!" Someone hollered out.

"Ya, Teri, stay in Dragon state," Jan Coaxed.

Camile had woke up and was laughing and clapping her little hand together.

The sound of the dragons returning victorious grabbed everyone's attention.

"Look, they're coming back! They have AlaHanDrea!" Jan yelled.

The dragons saw the charred remains of a human and knew there was more to this story than just reaching AlaHanDrea.

The sight of Teri stopped everyone in their tracks.

Danalli smiled so big when he saw his little girl.

"I'm a daddy! Wow, I really am a daddy!"

He ran over to Teri and gave her a great big hug.

"Let me look at you, baby girl... Wow! You are amazing! So, this is what a human dragon looks like! Beautiful!" He told his daughter.

"Oh daddy!" She said, then hugged him back.

They told the guys about the attempted kidnapping. It only took Braynar a minute or two to recognize the accomplices. They were caged for questioning.

The men gathered together to discuss the situation....

"Well, aren't you just the prettiest little thing I've ever seen!" AlaHanDrea told Teri.

"Thank you, Queen Ala Han Drea."

Jan looked confused and whispered to Teri, "why did you say her name like that?"

"Because she has 3 names. Ala is her first name, Han is her second name and Drea is her third name," Teri explained.

"Very good, Teri. How did you know my name?"

"Because I've dreamed about you my entire life."

"You have?"

"Yes ma'am, I sure have. When I'm full grown, you and I are going to be best friends. We will fight together and play together, too.

Once I'm grown.

I have much to learn from you... I'm so glad that I found you!

You're not that much older than me, ya know. You're still a teenager, too."

"Yes, I know."

"Really?" Jan said with excitement in her voice.

"Yes Jan, I'm only a few years older. I'm 19."

"Oh wow! I didn't know that! Teresa is older than you. By the way, where did Teresa go and why isn't she coming back?"

"Sweetie, Teresa drowned."

"I know, I was there, I saw her! I also saw that angel make her alive again, so why did he take her?"

"Because, under the law, she now belongs to him. He brought her back from being dead. She's his."

"Oh. Well, in that case, I belong to him and the baby belongs to the Bonner sisters."

"Did he make you alive again?"

"Yes, he sure did!"

"Well, according to the law, he can claim you, if he wants to, but you're too young for him to want to."

"But, Teresa is still a virgin."

"Not anymore, she's not. I can promise you that."

"Is that why he took her?"

"Probably. That's what most men want from a woman. At least every man I've ever ran across has wanted to do that. I just don't allow it... Not with all of them..."

"Oh, so Teresa is like his toy."

"Ya, pretty much. But, it beats dead!"

"Braynar is so sad without her! And he says I'm too young."

"You won't always be too young. Use this time to endear yourself to Braynar. He is an awesome man dragon! Learn from him. Become his student.

You girls need to go to bed and get some rest. It's almost daylight! Come on, off to bed with ya!!! You have a big day ahead of you! Now, get some sleep!"

Don't miss out!

Visit the website below and you can sign up to receive emails whenever Jeri Andrew publishes a new book. There's no charge and no obligation.

https://books2read.com/r/B-A-YGIAB-TBLQC

BOOKS 2 READ

Connecting independent readers to independent writers.

About the Author

Retired, I now spend my time writing stories from my imagination, to share with others, to help carry them away to another world, a world of magic and intrigue...